THE
GOLDEN STONE
JULES MARRINER

If you feel strongly about
supporting creative story making:
PATREON.COM/JULESMARRINERBOOKS

My website:
julesmarrinerbooks.com
for waffle and twaddle.
please share.

For a limited time, you can download

for **FREE**

julesmarriner.wixsite.com/landing-page

This book belongs to

Elliot

happy reading!

Jules

3

Chapter One

It wasn't the first time that Alfie had a sick, creepy feeling in the middle of the night. It was as if a venomous snake had curled up in his stomach. He opened his bedroom door and stuck his head out into the unlit hallway. The house was silent. He crept out, stepping over the floorboard that always creaked. On the landing he stopped dead, listening again to see if he could hear anybody.

Not a sound.

A shaft of moonlight fell onto the stairs making the crimson carpet appear silvery and grey. There was a hum coming from the kitchen; it grew louder as he approached. He knew what the sound was; it was like a beacon guiding him in the darkness. He found his way across the kitchen floor and reached out and felt a cold flat surface. There was a handle; he put his fingers on it and pulled. As he did so, a brilliant light flooded the kitchen and made Alfie wince.

The hum stopped as the fridge opened.

Now he could see what to take upstairs for his midnight snack.

He knew he had to be quick and quiet. He had to choose something that didn't require the opening of packets or crunching or crumbs. The fridge was his mum's territory and she would be super cross if she knew what he was up to. He really didn't want to be found out.

The fridge was loaded with fruit and vegetables; there was broccoli, carrots, lettuces and half a cucumber, red apples, green apples and some blueberries. Behind the sweet potato was half a tin of apricots, but Alfie didn't want any of those.

He knew exactly what he wanted and where it was.

Alfie weaved his hand through the assault course of vegetables and managed to move the jar of what looked like white worms; Sauerkraut. Totally revolting! Some kind of vinegary nastiness that Dad had once made him eat in a blind taste test. As his hand navigated around the container, he was being as quiet as a mouse on a mission. At last his hand touched the very thing he was after.

Cheese.

He pushed some of the other items away so that he could remove the Cheddar without too much difficulty. But then, something caught his eye. It was a colour that he didn't associate with the fridge. Something gold was shining right at the back.

"Odd," he muttered. He took the broccoli out and laid it on the kitchen table and did the same with the bag of carrots and the cucumber.

At the very back of the fridge was a strange golden oval shape, about the size of a chocolate Easter egg. Alfie reached out his fingers to touch it. It was cold like a copper pipe in winter and just as solid. He tried to roll it toward him, but it wouldn't budge.

"I wonder what on earth this is?" he asked himself.

"It's the Golden Stone," said a voice from behind him.

Alfie whirled around to see who was there in the darkness and saw a shadowy outline in the corner of the kitchen.

"Who's there?" Alfie demanded, his chest ready to burst with dread.

"It's ok, don't be scared. I'm here to help," said the shadow.

"Help...with what?" Alfie's voice squeaked.

"The Golden Stone," said the voice calmly. Alfie's eyes searched the darkness for a clue to the owner of the voice.

"Who are you?" Alfie asked again. "And what's that thing in my fridge?"

"It's a bit of a long story."

"Ok," said Alfie trying to buy some time, "I'm listening." He took a gulp of breath and tried to gather his courage.

"Why don't you shut the fridge and we can talk. I'm getting cold."

Alfie realised that he was beginning to shiver from the cold air wisping up from behind him too. The figure moved into the room a bit more and Alfie could see by the moonlight that the voice belonged to a boy about the same age as himself. He was wearing a t-shirt and gaping jeans ripped across the knee. His hair was spiky on the top and flattened down on the sides. Alfie couldn't see the boy's face; it was in shadow.

"My name is Star," said the boy.

"That's a weird name," said Alfie relaxing now he could see the boy.

"It's not weird where *I* come from," said Star. "Anyhow, my name is the least of our worries. I really need your help. The Golden Stone was stolen and it has to go back in its rightful place and time is running out!"

The words tumbled out in a jumble.

"Whoa, slow down! What is this 'golden stone'? and talk quietly; you'll wake my family up."

"Ok," Star whispered, "have you've heard of Black Wolf Manor?"

"Of course. Everyone knows that place. That big old house up on the cliffs that looks like it's about to fall into the sea. It's supposed to be haunted. Not even the man who does the Island Ghost Walk goes up there."

"There's a good reason for it," said Star turning slightly in the moonlight so that Alfie could see his face. His eyes were wide and his skin as white as the kitchen tiles. An earring glinted.

"You see - and this might sound a bit odd - but the manor is a bit like a plug. Underneath is some sort of geological phenomenon. A sort of whirling vortex." Alfie snorted involuntarily, but Star went on. "The manor was built hundreds of years ago to stop a huge hole appearing and everything around falling in. They say it was designed using magic and should last forever if it wasn't for that evil man Dreggs."

"Dreggs?" Alfie scratched the back of his ear. He knew he had heard the name before.

"Orville Dreggs, of Dreggs Development."

"Oh, yes, I know. He's builds houses. Massive new complexes with swimming pools and stuff. He's supposed to be building a new sports arena too for kids to do free activities. Archery and stuff. I like archery."

Star's eyes grew even wider.

"No! Don't fall for his twaddle! He's going to ruin the island forever."

"Oh come off it! This is all a bit unreal, isn't it?"

"You have to believe me! It's a matter of life and death!!"

"Shhh!" said Alfie, worried that someone might hear as Star's voice rose. "He's only building over the top of an old factory. That can't do any harm."

"You don't know what he's capable of. He's a megalomaniac; he thinks he can take over the world and build his horrid holiday parks everywhere. And he's starting with the Isle of Wight!"

Chapter two

When Alfie woke the next morning, he thought he'd had a strange dream. He was just thinking to himself about Mum saying cheese gives you nightmares, when he heard a sudden commotion from down stairs.

"Mu-um!" Matilda was screeching. Alfie imagined his sister's lip pouting in that unattractive way which she was so good at. "Jesse has put my shoe in the bog!"

Alfie wandered into the kitchen yawning and rubbing his fingers through his slightly tangled brown hair. His little brother Jesse was in his high chair flicking porridge at the walls. Another normal school morning.

"Morning Alfie," said Dad holding up a dripping shoe with the end of his index finger.

"Where's Mum?" asked Matilda trying to pull her long hair into a pony tail, "I can't go to school in odd shoes."

"Your mother is talking to the milkman and you can wear your purple shoes."

"You are joking!" said Matilda in a huff. "Purple shoes with my brown school jumper? That's gross! Anyway, I'll get a detention. It's not school uniform."

"It's ok; I'll write you a letter. Do you want some toast Alfie?" Dad turned wearily to Alfie.

"No thanks, Dad, I'm going to have some cereal." Alfie poured himself a bowl of cornflakes and sprinkled some sugar on top. He opened the fridge and reached inside for the milk.

The Golden Stone twinkled at him.

In a flash, the conversation from the night before came flooding back to him. He hadn't been dreaming. There really had been a boy in his kitchen and there really was a large golden orb at the back of the fridge. He looked at it and then at his teenage sister sitting at the kitchen table.

"What?" she said scowling, her lips pursed together like a cat's bottom.

"Nothing," he said. "Just wondering if you needed anything out of the fridge."

"Nope."

Alfie shut the fridge and went back to his bowl. He noticed the glass of orange juice in front of her. *So she'd been in the fridge, but not seen anything out of the ordinary. Either she was being very unobservant or else she really couldn't see it.*

Alfie decided to try something out.

"Dad, could you pass me the jam out of the fridge?"

"Crikey, what did your last slave die of?" Dad grumbled as he opened the door and poked about looking for the jam. "Anyway, jam on cornflakes? You really have got strange tastes."

Evidently, neither Dad nor Matilda had spotted anything unusual, despite the glaringly obvious golden glow escaping every time someone opened the fridge door. How mysterious. Alfie spooned a blob of jam onto his cereal. It tasted pretty good. Jesse threw his bowl on the floor and shrieked with giggles.

The front door opened and Mum came in with three bottles of milk.

"Mum, Jesse put my shoe in the loo. It's ruined," Matilda immediately whined.

"Oh it'll be ok, I'll give it a good scrub. Naughty Jesse, you mustn't put Tilly's shoe in the toilet." Mum opened the fridge door and rearranged some of the food so that the bottles could go in. The dazzling light from the fridge lit up her face. She didn't appear to notice anything strange. Alfie's Mum scrutinised the fridge everyday – he was sure if anyone was going to notice a great big gold rock in the fridge, it would be her.

"Hurry up Alfie, you'll be late. Don't stand there gawping at me," she said, doing three things at once.

Alfie gathered his coat and school bag and with a shout of goodbye, headed out of the door and off to school.

The island only had four schools and luckily, Alfie's was only a ten minute walk away. Being a relatively small place, the people mostly knew each other, even if only by knowing their cousin or auntie. Alfie wondered if he ought to ask around about Star. It wasn't a very *usual* sort of name; surely somebody would know him. He was really finding it very hard to know what to make of it all.

Firstly, who was Star and how did he get into the kitchen? Secondly, what did he want Alfie to do? And thirdly, how come nobody had noticed the Golden Stone in the fridge? It was too big to miss. It glowed. And thirdly again, what did it have to do with Dreggs Development?

Alfie was beginning to remember that he had heard Jesse moaning and Mum had got up to see to him just as Star was about to explain more. Star had disappeared into the shadows again, and had somehow got out of the house. Alfie had waited for the house to be quiet again and then crept back up to bed, a small piece of cheese in his hand. He looked down at his hand, half expecting to still see the cheese there.

"Psssst," came a noise. Alfie looked up. There, behind a bush, was a spiky haired boy in frayed jeans and t-shirt. Now in plain daylight, Alfie noticed how pale the boy was. He looked like he needed a dose of good healthy sunshine and a lungful of fresh air.

"Over here," motioned Star.

Alfie looked around and as no one else was watching, he wandered over.

"I've been waiting for you." Star whispered.

"What's with all the secrecy?" asked Alfie.

"I don't know really, I mean it's not as if anyone can see me!" Star said in his normal voice and stepped out from crouching in his hiding place.

"What do you mean?" asked Alfie.

"Haven't you worked it out yet? I'm your imaginary friend." Star threw his arms wide and twirled around.

"Right," said Alfie in disbelief. He was beginning to think this boy was a complete nutter.

"You don't believe me, do you?" said Star, stopping.

"Funnily, no. I'm twelve years old, not two. You must have mistaken me for my baby brother."

"I'll prove it to you." Star looked around him. A woman with a square silk scarf folded into a triangle was walking toward them. It was Alfie's next door neighbour, Nosy Nora. Before Alfie could stop him, Star sprinted toward her and just as she passed him, he hooked the scarf off her shoulders and flung it up into the air. It floated like a parachute to the ground. Nosy Nora turned in surprise and picked her scarf up, muttering to herself.

"Hullo Alfie – did you see that gust of wind? it was like a mini tornado - could've knocked me right off my feet," she said as she approached him. Alfie nodded mutely at her. She rolled her eyes as if to say 'tut tut, weather! eh?' as she plodded on.

"She didn't see you!" he whispered in amazement as she disappeared around the corner, his eyes like saucers.

"That's because only you can. I'm imaginary," Star proclaimed, matter-of-factly, leaning his shoulder on the nearest tree and folding his arms.

"Hold on a minute, my life has suddenly gone a bit weird. An imaginary boy tells me about a house that plugs the vortex on the cliffs; the stone that will stop the house falling into the hole is at home in my fridge, where no one else can see it?" Alfie looked at Star for confirmation.

"Got it in one," said Star. "You have to believe me," he said unfolding his arms imploringly, "because if Black Wolf Manor falls down, it's not just the house that will fall into the vortex – the whole of the island will."

"The whole island?" Alfie was suddenly alarmed.

"Black Wolf Manor is just the plug. If *that* goes, the whole of the island will disappear. All the houses, all the hills, all the people. Everything will disappear into the middle of the earth. Like going down a whopping plug hole."

Alfie studied his feet, his eyebrows knitting together.

"Look, I have to go to school," he said feeling muddled. "This is all a bit much to take in. Anyway, I'm not sure if I believe you."

"Look it up on the internet then – and check out the council's planning page," Star called back as he headed for the bushes again. "Dreggs Development wanted to buy vast amounts of land to build their holiday homes on, but the council rejected them. You see if I'm right!"

With that, Star disappeared behind the bush again and was gone. Alfie scratched behind his ear, slung his school bag over his shoulder and started off toward his school again.

Chapter three

www.dreggsdevelopment.com

Alfie waited for the computer to bring up the page and sure enough, Dreggs Development had a flashy website. On the home page, there were photographs of pale blue seas and white sandy beaches, sunshine and ladies in small bikinis and a large picture of a hollow faced man with a pencil thin moustache and a cheesy grin.

Alfie clicked the button that said 'Future Developments'. More pictures of holiday destinations in the sun, all with huge, posh looking hotels butting up to blissful beaches. Some of the hotels had swimming pools half the size of a football pitch; one had a simulated ski run with fake snow. It all looked *very* expensive.

Dreggs Development is proud to announce the opening of our new complex in the Seychelles.

Each holiday apartment will have its own Jacuzzi, a natural fish tank with live sea creatures and private beach.

Residents will have access to services such as turtle skin foot buffing, whole body wrinkle transformation and acid-rain wart removal.

Choose whatever you want to eat from our fully air conditioned restaurant (centrally heated when the temperature drops below 30°) – whether it's deep fried rhino ears, lightly steamed dolphin or crispy green turtle necks, our reputable chefs will be pleased to oblige.

Alfie let out a breath that he'd been holding while reading. It really did seem like there was more to Dreggs Development than met the eye. He checked the council website, and just as Star had said, Dreggs had been turned down. In fact, there were eighteen rejections for plans to build on the island in the last two years. Alfie didn't know much about planning, but that seemed like a lot.

Alfie turned back to his project. The topic this term was all about saving the environment. The class had already had a trip to the landfill site, where they had seen the sights and smelled the smells. He learnt that the island was actually quite good at recycling, but the rubbish mountain was still absolutely enormous and smelt like rotten onions.

It just so happened that the next part of the topic was about town planning and designing eco-friendly buildings. Miss Shufflebottom, the teacher, was giving out information about under-floor heating and solar panels.

"Do you know anything about Dreggs Development, Miss?" asked Alfie.

"Yes, they are the company that's hoping to build the new sports arena, aren't they?" said Miss Shufflebottom.

"I think so. Do you know anything about Mr Dreggs?"

"Oh yes, lovely man. I met him once at a Lord Lieutenant's 'do'. He was so charming and attentive. He really did make the evening for me."

Miss Shufflebottom sighed and had a dreamy look in her eyes. She blinked a few times. Alfie tried to read her expression, but it was rather foreign to him. She snapped suddenly back to reality and her cheeks blushed pink.

"I'm sure a sports arena will be a huge benefit to the community," she said, pulling herself together. "It'll probably save boys like George Spratt from a life of crime. I expect he'll join the boxing club. Roll on Dreggs Development, that's what I say. It's not a moment too soon."

Alfie chewed on the end of his pencil, mulling over what Miss Shufflebottom had said. Everyone thought the arena was a great idea. After all, at the moment the site Dreggs wanted for the arena was just a tangle of brambles. What harm could it do?

"I'll tell you the harm," hissed Star in his ear. It made Alfie jump.

"Oh crumbs, not only are you 'imaginary', you're reading my thoughts as well!" hissed Alfie.

Star ignored him. "Orville Dreggs has bribed someone in the government; he's got the go ahead for re-building if it's on a massive scale."

"How do you mean?" asked Alfie, trying to look like he was inconspicuously muttering at the computer.

"Like if there was a freak hurricane or flood and they needed to house people quickly - he has the main contract for the island re-development. When Dreggs pulls down the manor and the island falls into the vortex, he's going to claim rights from the government for re-building. I've seen the paperwork. It's all there in black and white."

Star sat back and waited for the information to sink in.

"And guess what he's going to build?"

"I don't know," said Alfie.

"This," said Star unrolling a large piece of paper.

Chapter four

Alfie found himself looking at a photocopy of an architect's drawing. There were lots of large buildings with huge glass sides and tall, slim trees planted into the walkways. The sketch showed couples laughing and children splashing in a man-made stream.

"I don't understand what this is," Alfie's brow furrowed.

"I'll tell you. It's a plan for a huge holiday complex. In fact, a Holiday Isle. He's going to use the bedrock of the Isle of Wight as the foundations. He's going to build homes, chalets and hotels for tourists and second home owners. But not the ordinary sort. For very rich people. Just think about it – what do we in Britain moan about the most?"

"Umm, too much homework?"

"No, no," said Star, "Put yourself in the shoes of an adult. What do they talk about all the time?"

"Cups of tea? Income tax?"

"No, no. Think...."

"The weather?"

"Right, so what sort of a holiday do most people want?"

"A beach one, hot sunny days and splashing about in the sea." Alfie slid a sideways look at Star.

"Correct. And what do we not have much of?"

"Hot sunny days and warm sea?" He was beginning to see where this was heading.

"Right. So exactly how much money do you think a person could make if he was able to make the beaches in the northern hemisphere warm and balmy, no matter what time of year it was?"

"Ok, hang on a minute. The weather is determined by nature. Surely you're not suggesting Dreggs can make *weather*?"

"No Alfie," Star shook his head miserably. "It's even worse than that. Look at this."

He passed Alfie a sheet of paper. It had 'Confidential' written in large red letters. It appeared to be a list of notes from the architect's plan.

It read;

1. Pipe work from Dead Sea; route to be decided. Feasibility study to be carried out to determine whether pipes should run over land or under sea. If overland, *will France mind*?

2. Source best deal for outdoor heaters for beach. See if China can make? Much cheaper if made by <u>small children</u>.

3. Source air conditioning for beaches in case of overheating in midsummer. (Unlikely).

4. Re-design pod for roofing -

"Pod for roofing?" Alfie looked at Star.

"He's going to build a huge glass roof over the whole island complex so that it's protected from the wind and rain in the winter. That's hundreds - no thousands - of sheets of glass!"

"So how are the plants and trees going to survive if they can't get rain?"

"He's going to lorry in water from the south coast reservoirs."

"Oh man, what a waste. And what's this about the Dead Sea?" asked Alfie, his finger poised over the first line.

"Oh, that a good one," Star nodded. "He wants to build a huge pipe from the Dead Sea, where the water is lovely and warm, and pump it to replace the water surrounding the island; then when you go for a swim, it'll be like swimming in the Mediterranean."

"But I thought the Dead Sea was full of salt," Alfie scratched his ear. "That's why it's Dead, nothing lives in it."

"Yup."

"So it'll kill off all our fish and stuff in our sea."

"Yup, and eventually run dry. Then the Dead Sea will be more of a Dead Desert and *our* sea will be as dead as a dead dog."

Alfie's horrified expression said everything.

"And you may notice," Star went on, "he's going to heat the air up on the beaches and then cool it down when it gets too hot. He wants it at the optimum temperature of 85° Celsius. Get this; he wants to ship in glaciers from the North Pole. Thousands of them. That's the only water they'll be able to drink when it melts 'cause the tap water will be ruined. He's going to be single handedly responsible for global warming *and* killing off all the Polar Bears."

"I don't get it, why would he do this?" Alfie's face screwed up in disbelief.

Star rubbed his thumb and two fingers together.

"Dosh. Wonga. Lolly. The pound signs must have lit up his eyes. Loads of people would rather not have to get on a plane these days, what with terrorists and huge queues and lost luggage. Anyway, it takes eight hours to get anywhere decent for guaranteed good weather. Who wants to take two whole days out of their holiday if they can avoid it? If they can just catch the ferry to the Isle of Wight to have a bit of sun, sea and starfish sandwiches, they will. He can basically charge what he wants, especially to the footballers and pop star brigade."

Alfie was beginning to get a very uneasy feeling in his tummy. Everything that Star was saying, although farfetched, was starting to stack up.

"I've got to think about this, Star," said Alfie, "where can I catch up with you later?"

"Oh don't worry about that," said Star. "I'll know when you want to see me again."

Alfie turned his back and stuffed his project work into his bag and as the bell rang, headed out to the canteen for lunch.

Chapter five

Alfie was confused. Star sounded like he was telling the truth. Why would he make up such an implausible story? Dreggs really did seem to be up to no good and needed to be stopped. But what could Alfie do? He was just a twelve year old school boy. How could he stand up to a big company like Dreggs Development, especially when Dreggs himself was seen as such a hero?

Alfie slumped on his bed, his arm flopped over the side and he shut his eyes. "Ok Star now would be a good time to talk," he muttered.

There was a disturbance coming from Alfie's wardrobe. Something banged from the inside; it sounded like someone was having a fight with his clothes. With an almighty crash, the doors flew open and Star fell out onto the floor, along with a hockey stick and a plastic box full of marbles, which scattered everywhere.

"Sorry," said Star sprawling, "got my wires crossed a bit. Did you want to see me?" He knelt up and crawled across the littered floor to sit on the edge of the bed.

Alfie looked at Star in astonishment. "How did you get in there? No, don't answer that! You just help me pick that lot up!"

"Yes-yes, in a minute, what I want to know is have you decided to *help* me yet?" Star rubbed his cheek with a grubby finger.

"Well, I admit that Dreggs sounds dodgy," Alfie confessed picking up a marble, "I just don't know what I can do to help. I'm just a kid."

"Just a kid? *Just a kid*! Are you mad?" Star jumped to his feet in astonishment and slipped on a marble. "You are the only person who can help," he said regaining his balance. "You have the Golden Stone in your fridge!"

"I was coming to that," Alfie scratched his ear, "I don't really get what the Golden Stone has to do with any of this, or what I am supposed to do with it or why it's in my fridge, or how it got there, or....well *anything*!"

"It's in your fridge because I knew you'd find it there. If I'd put it in the shed or the bathroom, you wouldn't have noticed it for months. I've seen how often you wash. It would have been too late. We've got to get it back before the weather turns."

"But what *is* it?" Alfie was getting impatient.

Star sat down on the bed again. He picked up a pencil and looked around for a piece of paper; he picked up a tissue box and started to draw on the back. "Ok, so you know when they build an arched bridge, like in the old days? The stone in the very middle at the highest point is the one that holds the bridge in place, right?" He pointed to the middle of the bridge that he'd just drawn.

"They call it a keystone, don't they?" said Alfie remembering his design and technology lessons.

"Right! If the keystone isn't there, the bridge falls down." He scribbled across the middle of his bridge and made an explosion noise. "Well, the Golden Stone is the keystone that holds Black Wolf Manor together, over the vortex. If it was just an ordinary building, it would crumble away eventually. The Golden Stone is said to have magical qualities that will hold the building in place forever. But just like a bridge, if there's no Golden Stone, there's no Black Wolf Manor."

"And at the moment, the Golden Stone is in my fridge....so what's holding the Manor house up?" Alfie asked, bewildered.

"Not a lot. The next breath of wind and it could go. It needs to go back into the gap before the weather gets bad; Dreggs will be watching the weather forecast."

"Cripes! So the manor would fall down and the whole island would be sucked into all that hot magma stuff, like you see coming out of volcanoes?"

Star nodded gravely.

"But how did the Golden Stone get from Black Wolf Manor to my fridge? Why did you bring it here?"

"It was that Orville Dreggs. He got one of his cronies to hack it out from above the entrance. His idea was that there would be this enormous environmental disaster; the Isle of Wight would disappear but he had to make sure it didn't look deliberate; otherwise the government wouldn't give him permission to build his wretched holiday isle. But the crook he got to do the work was as bright as midnight. He tried to sell the Stone on eBay. I heard whispers about what was happening, bid for it and won it. I have to say, it did look like an Easter Egg without the packaging; I guess most people thought I must be crazy paying *that* much!"

"Then what?"

"I had to hide it somewhere and I had to find someone brainy to help me."

"But I'm not brainy. I'm not in the top set for anything and I even get spellings wrong in algebra."

"Alfie," Star turned to him and looked him straight in the eye. "You are exactly what the world needs. Just 'cos you're not great at stuff at school doesn't mean you're a thicko. You think quickly and have no fear. That's everything I need to help me stop this situation from becoming a world catastrophe. I'm asking you – no, I'm begging you, please help."

Alfie put his head on one side.

"So why can't you do it?"

Star looked at his hands in his lap.

"I can't. And I can't tell you why I can't... I just can't."

Chapter six

"How about it then Alfie?" Mum was pouring dried pasta into a pot of boiling water.

"What?" Alfie looked up from the laptop, aware that he hadn't been listening. In fact he hadn't been listening to anyone since his last conversation with Star.

"It'd be nice to go to the mainland and stay at Auntie Linda's tomorrow, you know, for the weekend. We can all go. Then you've all got a cousin each to keep you occupied; it's been ages since I saw my sister and Dad can talk to Uncle Derek about motorbikes. You like it at Auntie Linda's don't you?"

Jesse was under the table eating a piece of carrot which had been there for a few days.

"Yum yum yum," he burbled.

"Yeah, I guess." Alfie was rather preoccupied with saving the planet and not really taking in what his mum was saying.

"Only, we need to set off on Friday afternoon. The weather forecast isn't very good for the weekend. There's supposed to be a big storm coming our way."

Alfie's ears pricked up. "Big storm?" he repeated.

"Eighty mile an hour winds or something. Don't worry; we'll be safely tucked up at Auntie Linda's cottage by then. And that's been there for three hundred years, so I can't see a bit of a wind making it disappear." Mum stirred the pasta.

Without saying another word, Alfie closed the laptop and hurried up to his bedroom. He paced up and down, kicking what was left of the marbles under his bed.

"Eighty miles an hour," he muttered to himself. "Crikey…that's a big storm…eighty miles an hour."

There was a tapping on his window. Alfie looked at his closed curtains. He was three storeys up. There were no trees outside.

What was tapping?

He slowly parted the curtain and peered outside into the gloom. There, with one side of his face pressed white against the glass and his fingers gripping the window frame, was Star.

"Could you please *open the flippin' window*." His voice rose.

Alfie unfastened the window and pulled the handle inward. Star fell into the room at Alfie's feet in a tangle of arms and legs.

"I'm going to have to practice landing," he said dusting himself down.

"There's a big storm coming," Alfie panted, ignoring Star's entrance. "That's bad, isn't it?"

"Yeah, that's really bad. You'd better get that Stone back before the storm comes."

"I can't," said Alfie. "My Mum's taking us to my Auntie's after school tomorrow."

"So do it tonight!"

Alfie shook his head.

"It's no good; my sister's having a sleepover. She's got nine girls sleeping in the living room. My Mum's making enough pasta to feed the armed forces. There's no way I can get out of the house without being noticed. They'll probably scream the house down if one of them hears me creeping around at midnight."

"Look Alfie, you have to find a way. Use your brain. I know you can do it. It's up to you now. I can't do any more."

"Why not? You got the Stone here, why can't you get it back in its hole?"

"Cos that darned Dreggs will be on the lookout for me." Star shut his eyes and rubbed the sockets with his palms. He was beginning to look anxious. "Just get the Golden Stone out of your fridge and up to Black Wolf Manor before that storm hits."

...

Alfie sat at the kitchen table, folded his arms and cradled his head. It was all getting a bit much. Just as he was coming round to the idea that he had to save the island and by association, the world, suddenly he was going to have to do it now. Not next week or next month. Not when he had built up enough courage or formed a good plan. Now. Before tomorrow night when the storm was due.

He was going to have to think of a good excuse to get out of going to Auntie Linda's – something that would convince Mum. Better still, if he could get her and the others to go to Linda's without him, at least they would be out of immediate danger if he didn't manage to get the Stone in.

"I need to think of a really cunning plan," he said.

"What?" said a female voice. "Who are you talking to Alfie?"

Alfie lifted his face and was confronted by a swarm of teenage girls all pressing themselves into the kitchen. The one who had spoken had long spidery eyelashes and, like a horse bothered by flies, kept flicking her hair. Alfie blushed deeply.

"Don't worry; it's just my silly little brother having a mad moment," said Matilda sniggering. "He often talks to himself – when he's not talking to action man or the vacuum cleaner. Come on, let's get something to eat. Mu-um?"

Mum came in from the garden with a basket full of washing.

"The pasta's in the pot, girls and there's garlic bread in the oven. Tuck in!"

Alfie returned to his room. He needed to think of how he could get out of going away tomorrow – and quick! Perhaps he could run away? No. Stupid idea, the police would be all over the island and would surely catch him. Maybe he could suggest he stays to look after the guinea pigs. No. Mum had probably already asked Nosy Nora to feed them.

He lay down on his bed. The pillow felt soft against his throbbing head. He pulled the duvet over his shoulder and despite his intentions, was fast asleep in minutes.

Chapter seven

There was a tap-tapping against his window. Alfie rubbed his eyes and yawned. Dull, yellow light was washing into the room. Tap tap, tappety tap tap. He pulled back the curtains, expecting to see Star clinging to the window sill again, but was met by rivers of rain drops racing each other down the pane. Trees in surrounding gardens were whipping back and forth and the sky had a foreboding quality.

Alfie stared at the weather. It was his worst nightmare and it had come early.

"Morning Alfie," said Mum as she stuck her head round the door. "You were a tired lad last night. I came and turned your light off at ten – you were sound asleep." She nodded at the window. "Looks like we'll need to take our wellies after all."

Alfie had a sudden flash of inspiration.

"I went to bed because I felt all hot and sick. I had to get up in the night and dash to the loo. Are those girls going to need the bathroom? 'cos I might need to throw up."

Alfie's Mum pushed the door open and took a few steps forward. She felt his forehead.

"You do feel a bit clammy," she said, "Don't worry, I'll tell the girls. Perhaps we shouldn't go today."

"Oh no, don't say that." fumbled Alfie, "I mean, I'd feel rotten about you not going to Auntie Linda's. It would be such a nice rest for you. Why don't you all set off early and have a lovely weekend?"

"Oh I don't know Alfie," murmured Mum, her brow creasing with worry. "I don't like the idea of leaving you on your own. What if you need something?"

"Nosy Nora could look in on me when she feeds our guinea pigs – I'm only going to be in bed anyway. It's not as if I'm going to need much looking after."

"Well..." Alfie could sense his mum was wavering.

"It's only for a couple of days. I'll be fine, honest. I promise I'll ring you if I get any worse. I'll put my mobile next to my bed. Really, I'd feel awful if you didn't go just because of me and my stupid stomach."

"Well..." Mum said indecisively.

"Auntie Linda loves looking after Jesse – she'd be gutted if you didn't go."

The thought of help looking after the kids seemed to make Alfie's mum's mind up.

"Ok," she said. "If you're sure you'll be alright. You stay in bed. No going on the computer all day, though. Just stay there and rest and I'll speak to Nora."

Alfie waited until she'd gone out of the room and then breathed a big sigh of relief. With parents at work and siblings out of the way, he could plan his next move. Only, he'd have to be careful that next door didn't see him. Nosy Nora would be bound to snitch.

With his hands on the window sill, Alfie looked out at the rain. His bedroom looked down over the town, across the slate roofs, now shiny, to the sea in the distance. He could just about make out through the gloom, the contour of Black Wolf Manor on the cliffs in the distance.

From downstairs Alfie heard the girls trooping out. He could hear his Mum shuffling them out, each with their overnight bags, back off to the parents in their Volvos, muffled goodbyes and then she shouted up the stairs.

"We're off Alfie - don't forget to ring me later. I'll call you tomorrow morning too. Just ask Nora if you need anything. Bye, love." Then the door slammed and there was silence in the house.

Alfie crept downstairs and into the kitchen. He checked that no one was left in the house and finding he was indeed alone, he slunk into the kitchen. There was an unbuttered piece of toast on a plate, probably left over from the girls' breakfast. It was a bit bendy, but he buttered it and spread jam on it none the less. He leant over the sink and looked out of the window to check the weather. It was still raining.

"This is bad!" said a voice in his ear.

Alfie dropped his toast in the bowl of washing up water and spun around.

"I do wish you would stop doing that!" he said, seeing Star peering out at the weather from right behind him.

"What?"

"Creeping up on me like some sort of ghost!"

"I can't help it! I just land wherever I can."

"Well, could you just announce yourself or something. A little noise perhaps?"

"What, like a fart?"

"I was thinking more of a cough!"

"Oh, right. I'll try and remember." Star picked the toast out of the bowl and started to eat it. "So, you managed to get rid of them?"

Alfie looked at the toast in disgust. "As far as I know, they are all going to Auntie Linda's after school. I am ill with a sicky bug and am staying in bed."

"Keep away from me then!" Star moved back a few paces.

"No, you wally, I'm not really ill, that's my plan for staying home. It'll be difficult for me to get out 'til later, though. Nosy Nora next door might see me and she'll be on the phone to Mum before I get to the garden gate."

"Right, so first we need a plan to get you out of the house." Star looked at his watch. "We really need to get a move on. Time is running away from us."

Chapter eight

Alfie spread out a map of the island on the floor. He smoothed it with a flat hand, but it was old and worn away across the creases.

"We are here," he said, his left index finger pointing to his road, "and Black Wolf Manor is here." He reached across to where the land poked out on a peninsula into the sea. There was one thin road leading up to it; he remembered from the school field trip last year, there were steep grassy hills on either side of the road which fell away into the tumultuous sea; at the very end was the Manor.

"It's a long trek. You'll need to get the Stone into a rucksack and sneak out soon," said Star.

Alfie checked the time; it was almost twelve o'clock. It seemed as though time had sped up. It was still raining – if anything it was heavier now than it had been earlier. The doorbell rang. Alfie and Star looked at each other.

Alfie opened the door a fraction and peered out. Star has deposited himself in the utility room, out of sight. Nosy Nora was battling with her umbrella and trying to stay upright. She was a grey haired lady of indeterminate age. She could be fifty or eighty, it was really hard to say. She was wearing a beige raincoat, silk scarf tied round her head in a triangle and wellington boots. She always wore the same clothing to walk her dog, summer or winter.

"Hello dear, just thought I'd see if you're alright?" She looked over Alfie's shoulder into the hallway as if half expecting to see evidence of wayward behaviour – a girl, for instance.

"Yeah, I'm ok thanks Nora. Just a bit tired. I'd invite you in, but..." he rubbed at his tummy and made a sickly looking face. It worked a treat.

"Oh, no dear. Anyway, I don't want to get my muddy boots all over your Mum's lovely laminate flooring. So you don't need anything? A tin of soup or some crackers? I could bring some over later for tea?"

"That's so kind, Nora, but really, Mum said I shouldn't eat anything 'til tomorrow. Just drink plenty of fluids, she said."

"Ah." Nora seemed disappointed. "What about the guinea pigs?"

"Well, if you wouldn't mind just covering them up before you turn in tonight, that would be a help. I should probably just go back to bed. I'm so tired," he stifled a fake yawn.

"That might be for the best, Alfie dear. I shall sort them out before dark and call on you in the morning. You know my number, you can always ring if you need something." With that, Nora turned and strode down the path, head down, umbrella forging a path through the driving rain.

"Thanks, Nora," called Alfie before shutting the door. "Well that's one obstacle out of the way. Now I just have to get out of the house without her seeing me."

"You'll be fine," said Star. "She falls asleep in her armchair watching the lunchtime news."

"How do you know that?" Alfie eyed Star suspiciously.

Star looked uncomfortable. "Oh I just, well, I just know."

Alfie didn't say anything; he waited for Star to continue. Alfie folded his arms.

"Don't ask, please. I can't say."

"Have you been spying on her? Have you been hiding in her cupboards or something?"

"Not exactly," said Star. "Let's just say I have sources."

Star threw Alfie his school back pack.

"Better go and get the Golden Stone. You don't want to forget the most important thing. And wear some waterproofs. It's raining."

That was an understatement. The rain was going sideways and there was a low hum each time the wind gusted. It seemed to come straight off the sea and hit the south facing windows.

Alfie went up to his bedroom and pulled some bags out of his wardrobe. In one bag was an old pillow, the other his costume from the school play. The third held his old waterproof trousers and coat. He pulled the trousers on over his jeans and hoiked them up. The coat was slightly too small, but there was little choice. It was wear this or get wet.

He went downstairs into the kitchen and opened the fridge door. He moved some of the food onto the table and for the first time had a good view of the Golden Stone. It really was something. It was a little irregular in shape, and sent out a magical glow even by the dim light of the refrigerator. He cupped his hands around each side and slid it towards him. As he lifted it from the shelf, he realised that although it felt very solid, it wasn't as heavy as he'd expected. Although it might be a different story, once he'd carried it on his back for eight kilometres.

Once the back pack was safely on and the straps tightened, Alfie tugged his hood up and drew the peak forward. He checked the laces on his walking boots; double knotted and ends tucked in. He took the torch from the kitchen drawer and put it in his coat pocket.

"So," he turned to Star, "I think I'd better sneak off down the garden and hop over the fence. We're less likely to be seen."

"*We*?"

"Aren't you coming too?"

"I can't, Alfie. I've done all I can. I've got to hand it over to you now. You're on your own. If Dreggs sees me about, he'll know something's up."

"But what about if Dreggs sees *me*? You didn't say anything about *Dreggs* being there."

"But he doesn't know you Alfie. Anyway, he won't be there. I'm just a bit jittery."

Alfie opened the back door. The wind fired a blast of rain into the kitchen. It soaked Alfie's face in fine mist instantly.

"Good luck, mate." Star patted Alfie's shoulder. "I have every faith in you."

Chapter nine

Alfie headed down the garden, keeping close to the hedge they shared with Nosy Nora. He pulled himself up onto their fence that led onto the playing fields, and with one last look back at his house, dropped over to the other side. No one else was daft enough to be out in the bucketing rain. The field was empty with the exception of a cat sheltering under a tree, who watched Alfie with some distrust as he trudged by. It was a good plan; the less people there were about, the less chance he had of bumping into someone he knew.

Coming out onto the main road, Alfie looked left and right. No pedestrians, just cars swooshing past, their tyres creating small waves onto the pavement. Head down, he made his way along the road away from the town. He thought he remembered a footpath that joined the road somewhere nearby which went through the woods and eventually up onto the downs – and although it was more exposed to the storm, it was a more direct route.

"Whoa there, me laddy," came a shout from behind him. Alfie turned, peeked from under his hood and with some horror, came face to face with a policeman. Water was trickling down his long craggy face, finishing with a drip on the end of his globular nose.

"Shouldn't you be at school, young man?" asked the policeman.

"I've got the dentist's," said Alfie feebly.

"Then you should have a pass from your teacher saying you are legitimately out of school." He held out his hand to receive the said document.

Alfie's jaw opened and shut.

"My brother flushed it down the toilet," he said. "He put my sister's shoe down there yesterday. It was her black school shoes. She had to go to school in her purple ones. She was really angry."

The expansion of the excuse seemed to give Alfie a bit of credibility.

"I see," said the policeman getting out his notebook. "I will still have to check with your school that you're out on genuine business. Name?"

Alfie grimaced at the policeman. The game was up. The school thought he was ill at home with a stomach bug and if a policeman rang because he'd been found strolling the streets, he'd be in really big trouble.

"Rootbeer," he said the first thing that came into his head.

"Rootbeer what?" asked the officer, writing in his book.

"Rootbeer Ferrari," said Alfie, watching a car go past.

"Darn this weather," the policeman shook some raindrops off his notebook. "And where do you live, Rootbeer?"

Alfie's mouth opened but nothing came out. If he gave his real address he'd be found out in no time, but in the heat of the moment, he couldn't think of a fake one. The policeman looked at him expectantly, pencil poised.

Suddenly, there was a crackling voice coming from the Police radio. He hooked it off his shoulder and listened to the message. The rain was spraying directly in his face, so he turned his back to speak back into the radio. Alfie saw his chance. Without waiting to see what the policeman would do next, he hared off up the road toward the woodland path.

Alfie didn't stop running until he was well into the woods. He leant against a huge oak tree and took some gasps of breath. There was no sign of anyone else, particularly, he was glad to see, the policeman. The path had turned into a muddy river, each step that Alfie took went 'squelch' and he realised he had left a nice trail for the policeman to follow, should he wish to.

The backpack was beginning to dig into his back. Alfie turned back to the path and although it was still raining, the weather didn't seem to be quite so bad. There were the occasional big plops dropping out of the trees and the floor was very soggy, but it wasn't as extreme as it had been in the street. He trudged on.

The trees way above his head threw themselves heftily from one side to the other, but down at ground level it was relatively calm. He listened to the song that the wind was singing and tried to whistle along. He wondered what Star was doing and if he might pop out from behind a tree any moment. Then he wondered if he was totally crazy, heading toward what could effectively, be an inside-out volcano.

He walked for what seemed to be the best part of an hour; it was beginning to get gloomy. Alfie couldn't be sure if that was because the weather was getting worse, or if it would be dark soon – he couldn't see the sky. The bag was hurting his back now. He took it off and slung it over his arm, although he could only carry it for a little while like that before it ached.

The wind tore a branch off a treetop in front of him. It didn't land – it kept going like a kite out of control until Alfie couldn't see it anymore. He pictured his mum, arriving at Auntie Linda's; Matilda with her face all screwed up as if she could smell something foul, and Jesse eating food from the dog's bowl. Dad would be sitting down with a glass of Uncle Derek's home brewed beer in one hand, getting in the mood for an evening discussing sprockets and throttle cables. It sounded like an enviable option to where he was heading.

At last, the trees thinned and Alfie could see the open view of the downs. He estimated it would probably be another half an hour's walk to get to the Manor. As he emerged, he realised just how much the trees had sheltered him. If anything, the wind had gained strength and as he strode along the narrow path on the top of the headland, he was buffeted from two sides, almost knocking him backwards. He leant into the gale and trudged on. The rain saturated his face and trickled down the front of his neck, like slimy eels.

"Oh man," said Alfie to himself, "I hope saving the world is worth it!"

There was dim light still in the sky as he rounded the bend, which at last led to Black Wolf Manor. It was a creepy looking place, with overgrown hedges and wind beaten trees hanging their bedraggled branches low over the long drive. One of the wrought iron gates hung feebly on it's hinges, the other was missing completely. Weeds grew ferociously among the shingle path, which at one time must have looked very grand. At the end was the sad looking manor house, flaking with years of neglect. The windows looked like dark gaping eyes; Alfie shielded his face with his hand and looked for the door. It was under an archway at the top of which was a large black gap. A gap where the Golden Stone should be. He would really like to just put it back and leave, pronto. He wasn't easily scared, but this place was something else.

Just then, he heard a shout, like someone trying to be heard above the din of the wind. It was hard to make out what was being said. Alfic leapt into the undergrowth, just as a man appeared from the side of the house.

He was zipping up his anorak over his large belly and saying something over his shoulder to someone out of view. Alfie felt a large drip run down his face; he wiped it away and even in the dim light, he could see it was blood. He must have scratched his face on the brambles as he's jumped.

The man stood under the archway.

"Bring the van round the front Lacey!" he yelled, louder than the din of the wind. "I know the boss said keep it out of sight, but I'm getting soaked. Just park it here by the door – it'll shelter us a bit while we wait."

A white van edged slowly round the side of the manor house, squeezing between an overgrown Buddleia and the brickwork. The rain gusted down on the windscreen but the wipers weren't fast enough to clear the deluge. He managed to park in front of the entrance, obscuring Alfie's view of the front door.

"Well that's done it!" said Alfie to himself. How was he supposed to get the Stone in place now? There were two burly men sheltering under it. And they were waiting for someone. Alfie thought perhaps they were waiting for Star. The 'boss' must be Dreggs; he assumed Dreggs hadn't told his employees what would happen to the building if the keystone wasn't put back. Alfie guessed that Dreggs hadn't told them very much at all; even two dim wits like that wouldn't hang around waiting to be crushed for a few quid.

There was still just about enough light to see where branches lay. Alfie pushed his way through the undergrowth toward what he assumed must be near the cliff edge. If he remembered rightly, there was a path that ran along the headland and joined the bottom part of the Manor garden. Hopefully it hadn't

81

been washed away by storms since his visit with the school.

At last, the thick woodland ended and there was nothing but the sea below him. He could see the white horses whipping against the rocks at the bottom of the cliff and hear the crashing sound they made a few seconds later. The chalky white path was still there, just. It was only as wide as he was, and then fell away to nothingness. One false step, one big gust of wind and he'd be gone. No one would ever know what happened to him, because no one knew he was here.

Alfie started to feel shaky. There was no one to rescue him, no one to help him. He was all alone. Whatever happened from now on was completely down to him.

He edged along the path, holding on to any branches that were within reach. The wind played a game with him, sometimes falling to a mere breeze, then blasting a gust that nearly took him off his feet. Everything was wet, the branches, the chalky path and the occasional bit of grass. It was completely dark now and Alfie had to use all his senses to get him along the path and out of immediate danger. Only the faint whiteness of the chalk helped him.

He was starting to feel a little confidence eek back into him, he was sure he was nearly by the gate to the gardens, when he slipped on some slick stones. His foot flew from under him and shot out over the edge of the cliff. They say that your life flashes in front of you at times like this, but to Alfie, it was more like he grew ten years older in that millisecond. His stomach flipped as adrenaline raced through him; his right arm waved wildly trying to get some balance.

Half of him was supported by thin air; he slammed down on the other knee and held on to the wispy branch of a tree with his left hand. In a split second, Alfie realised the branch didn't feel like it could take much weight and might break at any second. There was no choice; he had to hope it would hold for another moment. He lurched forward and grabbed hold of anything he could feel in the darkness. The branch snapped like a firecracker just as his hand grasped something solid. A wooden post. A gate!

Alfie pulled himself toward it and shoved it open. He collapsed into the garden and lay on the wet grass, gasping for breath. He lifted his head and looked back to where he had been. In the dark he could make out the path and the gate; beyond that a whole lot of nothingness. Pitched down into the angry sea and eroded by the storms, the path vanished. If Alfie hadn't slipped, he would have stepped into thin air and been drowned by the waves below.

Chapter ten

Having stopped shaking quite so violently, Alfie decided to cross the garden, lit not by moonlight, but by a weird sort of luminescence. He wanted to see if he could access the front from any other way. Perhaps he could wait until the men had gone home; then, he could sneak out and replace the Stone. A gust of wind blew some freezing rain into his face, but something more alarming caught his attention. The ground had seemed to shake slightly as the wind blew hard. Like a lorry was driving past. But then there was another noise. The house creaked loud and long. It was the sort of sound you might expect to hear right before a house collapsed to the ground like snowflake made of lead. There would be no time to wait for the men to leave; he'd have to do something pretty soon, before it was too late.

Alfie heaved his backpack over his shoulder and started off across the slippery grass, aiming to circumnavigate the ornamental rose bed in the middle of the garden. Suddenly there was a shout above the roar of the wind.

"Boy!"

Alfie whirled around. Behind him was a man in a long wax raincoat, wearing a leather cowboy hat. The rain was dripping off the brim and rolling down his coat. It was not one of the men from the van.

"You, boy! Stop right where you are!"

Alfie was so terrified and surprised that he did what he was told as the man strode toward him. His legs had turned to stone and there was little hope of getting them to obey the command to run. The man grasped Alfie's shoulder with one hand and pushed his cowboy hat further up his face with his other index finger.

With some horror, Alfie realised who this was. Hollow face; pencil thin moustache. It was Orville Dreggs.

"So, come to ruin my plans, have you? I knew I'd need to be here myself to stop Star or one of his skivvies!" he snarled. Gone was the charm that Miss Shufflebottom had apparently seen. Alfie's shoulder was hurting under Dregg's grip.

"Nothing to say for yourself, you little runt? So where is he?" Dreggs looked around. "Too scared to come himself, so he sent someone dispensable. What have you got in the bag, sonny? It seems a little heavy!"

"Get off me you bully," shouted Alfie, getting his voice back and pulling away. "I know what you're trying to do – but believe me, it won't work." Alfie swung the bag off his shoulder and shoved its weight straight at Dreggs. It caught him in the stomach and threw Dreggs off balance. He landed in a heap on the sodden grass. Alfie didn't wait to see him get up.

"Cagney! Lacey!" Alfie heard Dreggs shrill scream. Alfie was halfway to the house when he saw the two oversized chumps come puffing round the corner.

"After him!" Dreggs screamed maniacally, pointing his thin finger towards Alfie. The men looked in horror at Dreggs and then anger at Alfie, who was within sprinting distance of the house. He could see in a split second there was no way past them, the path was too narrow. He'd have to try the other side, which had no obvious path at all. Maybe there'd be a gate, he hoped. Without further delay, Alfie hurtled towards the house, his eyes scanning for an escape route.

With the men's footsteps behind him, Alfie realised to his horror there was no gate. The house ended in a high wall with a spiky bush growing up it. He quickly checked the windows, but most of them were boarded up. Except for one small hole in the brickwork; it was the size of a sofa cushion. It must have been a coal chute at one time. He didn't wait to find out what its purpose was; he shoved the bag inside and followed head first.

He thought he'd made it, but just as he slid down into the black hole, one of the men caught his foot.

"Gotcha!" Alfie heard from the other side of the wall. With fear pumping in his chest and pain where the man had grabbed his ankle, he pulled with all his might and then kicked back toward the man. He felt his foot come into contact with something quite solid and then he was released.

"Aw flamin' eck! The little yob broke me nose!"

Alfie knew there was no way that any of the men outside could follow him down the chute because it was only just wide enough for him to squeeze down. He felt in his pocket for the little torch and flicked it on. In the dim light he realised he was indeed in a coal cellar, although there wasn't any coal left; just a lot of spider's webs and dust. He noticed a door on the other side of the room and to his relief when he turned the handle, he found himself in what used to be the kitchen.

He had a quick look around to try and get his bearings and saw the back door. It had two glass panels looking out onto the back garden. The rain beat down on the glass and for a moment he was transfixed.

Then a demented face reared up on the other side; with a mouth wide open and spit clinging from top lip to bottom, Dreggs howled at Alfie some vile and unrepeatable words. The door knob rattled, but to Dreggs's consternation, the door stayed locked.

"Lacey, get me something to smash this damn glass!" he screeched.

Alfie didn't wait to see. He grabbed his bag and ran out of the kitchen and straight up the stairs in front of him. Perhaps there'd be somewhere to hide upstairs. He knew he couldn't go to the front door – Cagney might be waiting for him.

A blast of air blew down the empty chimney; the house groaned. Alfie ran into the first room he came to, slammed the door and turned the key in the lock; the first bit of luck he'd had.

The room was empty. There was nowhere to hide. The bare, dusty floorboards ran from wall to wall. Wallpaper was peeling from the corners and there was a damp musty smell – like wet clothes left in a washing machine for too long. But at least there was glass in the windows. He looked out. Outside was the front of the house; the trees and bushes were thrashing in the wind and drooping from the weight of the rain. Directly underneath him was the roof of the white van.

The house let out an enormous jolt and the walls moaned loudly. It was as if someone had whipped out a table cloth from underneath, in some sort of macabre magic trick. Alfie almost lost his balance. He frantically considered what he could do. Could he save his own life? Let alone the lives of the population? If he didn't do something pretty soon, the house would fall down the hole and take with it all of them and the Stone. Alfie wished Star could be here to tell him what to do.

There was a sudden bang-bang-bang as someone took the stairs two at a time.

"Where are you boy?" yelled the voice of Orville Dreggs. "I'm gonna rip your legs off and feed them to some crocodiles!"

Alfie scanned the room. There must be something that could help him. He looked at the window. The house shuddered as another squall hit it front on. There was only one thing he could do; put the Stone back.

Chapter eleven

Alfie opened the window. It was stiff from years of being shut, but at least it wasn't locked. The rain shot in from outside, wetting the floorboards instantly and the strength of the wind pummelled the side of Alfie's head. He braced himself against it and threw a leg out onto the window sill. He ducked under the window and forced the rest of his terrified body to follow his leg, and at the last minute, turned and grabbed the bag with the Golden Stone in it. The van roof was some drop from the sill, but Alfie thought he could probably do it. He swung the bag over one shoulder and lowered himself, clinging, until his drenched fingertips slipped on the slick windowsill and he plummeted the last few feet .

Just then, two things happened. Dreggs broke through the door and Cagney and Lacey looked up as they heard Alfie thump onto their van.

"Come back here you thug!" screeched Dreggs as he stuck his head out of the window above Alfie, rain battering his face.

"I've got him guv," said Cagney, his bloodied nose flattened as he tried to grab Alfie by the ankle. Thankfully the van was too tall for the man to be able to get at him and Alfie kept out of the way of his waving arms.

The house sighed and shifted violently. The men and Alfie were all knocked over. Alfie clung on to the roof, his knuckles white, then struggled to his feet as soon as the quake had stopped, faster than the boneheads who were still reeling on the ground. He unzipped his bag and retrieved the Stone, which even in this weather, shone like a diamond.

"He's got the Golden Stone!" shrieked Dreggs rabidly, "I knew he was up to something! Get him before it's too late!"

Cagney made a wild swing again, but Alfie stamped his foot, just catching fingertips under his boot. The man howled in pain. Then there was another noise; it sounded like a thunderstorm underneath the ground. In one terrible flash of realisation, Alfie knew that the house was about to cave in; he had seconds, if that. He bounded forward with the Stone in his hands, knowing that he'd have to launch himself up and toward the hole – the van didn't quite reach. There was no time for wondering what might happen if he missed – he leapt...

And in that moment, something amazing happened. It was as if the Stone was magnetic and was being drawn back toward its rightful place. There was no way that Alfie could miss because he was no longer in control. The Stone shot back into the hole above the door with Alfie still attached to it, almost trapping his fingers in the brickwork. As he let go there was an almighty clap of thunder and a flash of the brightest lightning you could imagine. He fell to the ground between the van and the house with a thump, and everything went black.

...

When he came to, Alfie was looking into the blurry face of someone he recognised. It was someone he couldn't place – he'd definitely met him recently, but he couldn't think where. Something to do with the bulbous nose. Then a drip of rain ran down it

99

and plopped onto Alfie's face and he remembered.

"Alright sonny, it's all over now," said the man crouching over him.

"Are you going to arrest me?" asked Alfie feebly.

"Arrest you?" chuckled the Policeman, "certainly not. You stopped these criminals from breaking the law. We don't normally arrest upstanding members of the public! I believe there was some sort of illegal shenanigans going on here tonight. We're been after these two witless numbskulls for some time, you know. As for that Dreggs..."

Alfie sat up. It was still drizzling a bit, but the wind had dropped enough to notice how quiet it now was. There were two police cars and a police van parked on the driveway to Black Wolf Manor. Two policemen were bustling Cagney and Lacey into the back of the van, while two others were handcuffing Dreggs who was busy cursing and frothing at the mouth.

"You sit here quietly for a minute while I assist my colleagues," said the Policeman.

Alfie rubbed his pounding head and felt the start of a large bump emerging.

"Well done Alfie, you did it!" said Star appearing from nowhere.

Alfie looked at him. "I nearly died! More than once!"

"Aw come on, you were great. Look, you've saved hundreds of people, if not the world and, I reckon, put Orville Dreggs behind bars! You're a hero!"

Alfie snorted. "Perhaps you'd like to tell me how the Police knew to come here. Did you ring them?"

"Yeah right!" Star used his hand as an imaginary phone to his ear. "Hi, my name's Star, I'm from the future and I'd like to report Orville Dreggs for pulling the plug out on the earth." I don't think they would have taken that too seriously. That copper with the nose just stalked your tracks along the muddy path. Followed his nose, so to speak," he tittered.

"What do you mean, you're from the future? I thought you were from my imagination?"

"Ah," Star looked awkward. "*That* sort of slipped out. Forget I said anything."

"I can't *forget* you said you're from the future!"

"Oh crikey, I am going to be in *big* trouble." Star looked like he was wrestling with what to say next. "Look, the thing is – it was my Great great Granddad, Albert Black that built Black Wolf Manor. He was a sort of magician. And I don't mean he pulled rabbits out of hats. He studied magic properly, like a wizard.

"Back in those days, he could have been thrown in prison if he'd been found out. He used to make potions to cure people of illnesses; he was like a pharmacist. Anyway, he was left this book by the old man who taught him and inside it showed a map of the ground under Black Wolf Manor. There was a description of how it was like a whirlpool under a volcano and that if the top layer of earth was disturbed, the surrounding countryside could be sucked in!"

Alfie listened intently. "Go on," he said.

"That dratted Orville Dreggs had a Great great Grandfather too. His name was

Phinosorus Dreggs. He knew about the vortex too and decided to give it a helping hand by scalping the top layer off the ground."

"Why would he do that?" asked Alfie.

"So that he could get rid of all the annoying peasants that lived here and he could have the entire island to himself. Trouble was, he didn't reckon on Grandpa Albert getting there first."

"So your great great Granddad built Black Wolf Manor to stop old Dreggs digging up the ground?"

"Yeah, and that's why he made the Golden Stone; with the help of a little magic, he made sure the building would last forever. So long as no one hacked it out and sold it on the internet!"

"I still don't get it," said Alfie. "If you really are real, how come no one else can see you?"

"Ah, well, that's Physics for you. I'm a sort of memory in reverse. I'd better not tell you exactly how it works, 'cos that'd be cheating. You're not supposed to invent time travel for another twenty five years. I'd best go – we'll meet again when you're a lot older. Good luck and don't forget to put a fiver on Brading Town winning the cup next year."

"Right, come on then," said the Policeman returning. Alfie looked up and saw him motioning toward his car. "In you get and I'll give you a lift home." Alfie looked back at Star, but he was gone.

"Where did you say you lived again, sonny?"

Chapter twelve

From the depths of his sleep, Alfie became aware that his ear felt wet. And it was as though something was pulling on it. He couldn't remember having a dog. Perhaps he'd gone to Auntie Linda's after all, and Arnie the Dobermann needed to be let out. He opened a bleary eye. He was definitely in his own bed. And it felt like he'd only just fallen into it moments ago, now he remembered - just after the policeman dropped him off at home.

Jesse's face loomed into focus.

"Aw my goodness Jess, get off chewing my ear!" slurred Alfie.

"Hi darling!" called Mum, peering around the door. "Are you feeling better now?"

"What time is it?" Alfie asked, his head flumping back onto his pillow.

Jesse slid off the bed and toddled up the hallway to find some other mischief.

"What are you doing home? Why aren't you at Auntie Linda's?"

"Well," said Mum, coming into the room, "the weirdest thing happened. We got there in good time yesterday lunchtime, had a lovely afternoon, had dinner and we all turned in early. But we were all woken by a ferocious thunderstorm – it seemed like the whole Earth shook. I've never known anything like it.

"Then, this morning when we got up, there was a colossal hole in the back garden! We couldn't believe it. Apparently there are loads of old wells on the moors where Auntie Linda lives and one just opened up *right in the middle of the marigolds!* She had no idea there was a well under her garden though. Uncle Derek was most annoyed. He was going to enter the local flower competition next week."

Alfie listened to his mum twittering on like a little sparrow, trying hard to take it all in.

"Anyway, we thought it would be too dangerous with Jesse, such a *big* hole – so we packed up and came home." She picked up Alfie's wet clothes and looked at them with gathering curiosity.

"So tell me, what *exactly* have you been up to?"

"Oh you know," said Alfie pulling the warm duvet up over his aching, bruised body. "Nothing much. Just saving the world."

THE END

40620164R00066

Printed in Poland
by Amazon Fulfillment
Poland Sp. z o.o., Wrocław